HOPSCOTCH

Cockerel's Big Egg

First published in 2004 by
Franklin Watts
338 Euston Road
London NW1 3BH

Franklin Watts Australia
Hachette Children's Books
Level 17/207 Kent Street
Sydney, NSW 2000

A CIP catalogue record for this book is available
from the British Library.

ISBN-10: 0 7496 5767 7
ISBN-13: 978 0 7496 5767 3

Series Editor: Jackie Hamley
Series Advisor: Dr Barrie Wade
Cover Design: Jason Anscomb
Design: Peter Scoulding

Printed in China

Franklin Watts is a division of Hachette Children's Books.

Cockerel's Big Egg

by Damian Harvey and François Hall

FRANKLIN WATTS
LONDON•SYDNEY

The farmyard is always busy.

The chickens need feeding.

The cows need milking.

The sheep need taking to the fields.

"It's too busy!" cried the Farmer.

"Something will HAVE to go!"

"Did you hear that?" clucked the Chickens. "Something has to go! But it won't be us, because we give eggs for the Farmer's breakfast."

9

"It won't be me," miaowed Cat.
"I chase the rats."

"Or me," baaed Sheep. "I give
wool for his clothes."

"It won't be me," mooed Cow.
"I give milk."

Everyone looked at Cockerel.

"I wake the Farmer up,"
crowed Cockerel.

But Cat shook her head. "The Farmer's clock wakes him up."

The Chickens laughed.

"You stupid Cockerel – thinking you woke the Farmer."

"Well, I crow and bring up the sun," crowed Cockerel.

But Cow shook *her* head.

"Sometimes the sun comes up

before you crow."

15

"You stupid Cockerel," clucked
the Chickens, "thinking you
brought up the sun!"
Cockerel hung his head.

17

Then Cat spoke again. "Cockerel makes sure you Chickens lay lots of eggs."

"RIDICULOUS!" laughed the Chickens, louder than before. "You must be as stupid as that Cockerel!"

But Cat told everyone that Cockerel could lay an egg big enough to feed the Farmer and all his family.

"And what would happen to you Chickens then?" miaowed Cat. "Chicken dinner, that's what!"

"Nonsense!" clucked the Chickens.
"Everyone knows that cockerels
can't lay eggs."
"Very well," miaowed Cat.

"We'll have a Big Egg competition. If Cockerel wins, you Chickens must stay in the shed to make room in the farmyard."

"But I can't lay eggs," clucked Cockerel. "Ssshhh!" purred Cat and whispered his plan.

That night Cockerel and Cat crept into the shed. "COCK-A-DOODLE-DOO!" crowed Cockerel.

The Chickens jumped out of their
nests in surprise.

"It's time to see who has laid the
biggest egg," miaowed Cat.

Everyone looked at the Chickens'
eggs. Then they went outside to see
Cockerel's egg.

And there, in the
middle of the pond,
was the biggest egg
they had ever seen.
They could hardly
believe their eyes.
Cockerel
had won!

The next morning, the giant egg had gone. But the Chickens stayed in the shed as they had promised.

So they never saw the Farmer take away the old tractor to make more room in the farmyard!

Hopscotch has been specially designed to fit the requirements of the National Literacy Strategy. It offers real books by top authors and illustrators for children developing their reading skills.

There are 21 Hopscotch stories to choose from:

Marvin, the Blue Pig
Written by Karen Wallace
Illustrated by Lisa Williams

Plip and Plop
Written by Penny Dolan
Illustrated by Lisa Smith

The Queen's Dragon
Written by Anne Cassidy
Illustrated by Gwyneth Williamson

Flora McQuack
Written by Penny Dolan
Illustrated by Kay Widdowson

Willie the Whale
Written by Joy Oades
Illustrated by Barbara Vagnozzi

Naughty Nancy
Written by Anne Cassidy
Illustrated by Desideria Guicciardini

Run!
Written by Sue Ferraby
Illustrated by Fabiano Fiorin

The Playground Snake
Written by Brian Moses
Illustrated by David Mostyn

"Sausages!"
Written by Anne Adeney
Illustrated by Roger Fereday

The Truth about Hansel and Gretel
Written by Karina Law
Illustrated by Elke Counsell

Pippin's Big Jump
Written by Hilary Robinson
Illustrated by Sarah Warburton

Whose Birthday Is It?
Written by Sherryl Clark
Illustrated by Jan Smith

The Princess and the Frog
Written by Margaret Nash
Illustrated by Martin Remphry

Flynn Flies High
Written by Hilary Robinson
Illustrated by Tim Archbold

Clever Cat
Written by Karen Wallace
Illustrated by Anni Axworthy

Moo!
Written by Penny Dolan
Illustrated by Melanie Sharp

Izzie's Idea
Written by Jillian Powell
Illustrated by Leonie Shearing

Roly-poly Rice Ball
Written by Penny Dolan
Illustrated by Diana Mayo

I Can't Stand It!
Written by Anne Adeney
Illustrated by Mike Phillips

Cockerel's Big Egg
Written by Damian Harvey
Illustrated by François Hall

The Truth about those Billy Goats
Written by Karina Law
Illustrated by Graham Philpot